Number One, Tickle Your Tum

A Red Fox Book: 0 09 943879 8

First published in Great Britain by The Bodley Head,
an imprint of Random House Children's Books

The Bodley Head edition published 1999
Red Fox edition published 2002

1 3 5 7 9 10 8 6 4 2

Red Fox Books are published by Random House Children's Books,
61-63 Uxbridge Road, London W5 5SA,
a division of The Random House Group, Ltd,
in Australia by Random House Australia (Pty) Ltd,
20 Alfred Street, Milsons Point, Sydney, NSW 2061, Australia,
in New Zealand by Random House New Zealand Ltd,
18 Poland Road, Glenfield, Auckland 10, New Zealand,
and in South Africa by Random House (Pty) Ltd,
Endulini, 5A Jubilee Road, Parktown 2193, South Africa

THE RANDOM HOUSE GROUP Limited Reg. No. 954009
www.randomhouse.co.uk

A CIP catalogue record for this book is available from the British Library.

Printed in Singapore

Number One, Tickle Your Tum

JOHN PRATER

RED FOX

Shall we play the

counting game?

Number one

tickle your tum.

Number two

just say 'BOO!'

Number three

touch your knee.

Number four

touch the floor.

Number five

do a dive.

Number six

wiggle your hips.

Number seven

jump to heaven.

Number eight

stand up straight.

Number nine

walk in line.

Number ten

start again.

What a clever

little bear!

Other Baby Bear books to collect:

Hold Tight!

Again!

Clap Your Hands

I'm Coming to Get You!

The Bear Went Over the Mountain

Walking Round the Garden

Oh Where, Oh Where?

The Big Baby Bear Book